Grizzly Riddles

by Katy Hall and Lisa Eisenberg

pictures by Nicole Rubel

Dial Books for Young Readers · New York

Dial easy-to-read

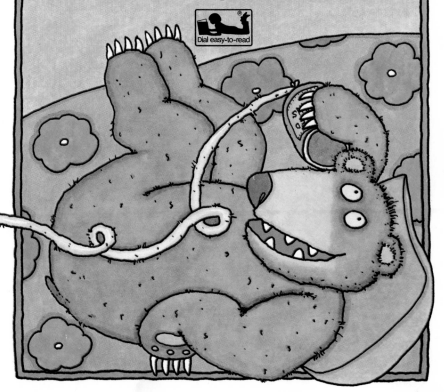

Published by Dial Books for Young Readers
A Division of Penguin Books USA Inc.
375 Hudson Street
New York, New York 10014

Library of Congress Cataloging in Publication Data
Hall, Katy. Grizzly riddles.
Summary: An illustrated collection of riddles and puns
about grizzly bears, such as "Why can't grizzlies
sing the high notes? They're all bear-a-tones!"
1. Riddles, Juvenile. 2. Grizzly bear—Juvenile humor.
3. Puns and punning. [1. Riddles. 2. Puns and punning.
3. Grizzly bear—Wit and humor. 4. Bears—Wit and humor.]
I. Eisenberg, Lisa. II. Rubel, Nicole, ill. III. Title.
PN6371.5.M396   1989   818'.5402   86-29275

First Hardcover Printing 1989
ISBN 0-8037-0376-7 (tr.)
ISBN 0-8037-0377-5 (lib. bdg.)
1 3 5 7 9 10 8 6 4 2

First Trade Paperback Printing 1992
ISBN 014-036116-2 (ppr.)
1 3 5 7 9 10 8 6 4 2

The paintings, which consist of black ink
and colored markers, are color-separated
and reproduced in full color.

Reading Level 2.3

To the three bears:
Grizz-leigh, Koala Kate,
and Annie-the-Pooh

K.H. and L.E.

To Richard

N.R.

What do little girl
grizzlies wear in their hair?

Bear-ettes.

What would you get
if you crossed
a grizzly and a kangaroo?

A fur coat with pockets!

What baseball team do grizzlies root for?

The Cubs!

What kind of fish
do grizzlies like to catch?

Bear-acudas!

What do you call
a nice, cheerful,
friendly, helpful grizzly?

A failure.

Why can't grizzlies
sing the high notes?

They're all bear-a-tones!

What happened to
the grizzly skater
who fell through the ice?

She became a blue-bearie!

Who is a grizzly's favorite funnyman?

Grrrrrrrowl-cho Marx!

Where do grizzlies
sit on airplanes?

Anywhere they want to!

Why didn't the grizzly
walk on the gravel road?

She had bear feet!

What time is it
when a grizzly wakes up
from his nap?

Time to run!

What is bigger than
a grizzly but lighter
than a feather?

A grizzly's shadow.

Why did the grizzly
cross the road?

It was the chicken's day off.

Why can't a grizzly keep
a secret at the North Pole?

His teeth always chatter.

What happens when a banana sees a grizzly?

The banana splits.

What grizzly stands in the middle of New York Harbor?

The Statue of Lib-bear-ty!

What time do grouchy
grizzlies get up in
the morning?

At the crank of dawn!

What weather is even worse
than raining cats and dogs?

Drizzly grizzlies!

Who won the grizzly beauty contest?

No one.

Where do grizzlies
come from?

Bear-izona!

What sport
do grizzlies love?

Picnic basket-ball!

When grizzlies make a pie, what do they like to put in it?

Their teeth!

Why was the grizzly
so smart?

She just ate
a whole school of fish!

What do you call
a bear with a new perm?

A frizzly grizzly!

What Broadway musical
do grizzlies like best?

My Bear Lady

Why do *you* look like
a grizzly cub
when you take a bath?

Because you're a little bare!

Why did the grizzly tip-toe
through the campsite?

He didn't want to wake up
the sleeping bags!

Why do grizzlies have
such sticky hair?

They use honeycombs!

What would you do
if a grizzly sat in front
of you at the movies?

Miss most of the movie!

Which grizzly
is the ringleader?

The first one in the bathtub.

What would you get
if you crossed a grizzly
with a dog?

A neighborhood without any cats!

What sound do grizzlies make when they kiss?

Ouch!

What do you get when
a grizzly walks through
your vegetable garden?

Squash!

Is it true that a grizzly
won't attack you at night
if you carry a flashlight?

It all depends on
how *fast* you carry it!

Why don't grizzlies
spend much time
in front of a mirror?

They can't bear it!

What should you do
if you see a great
big, hungry grizzly?

Hope he doesn't see you!

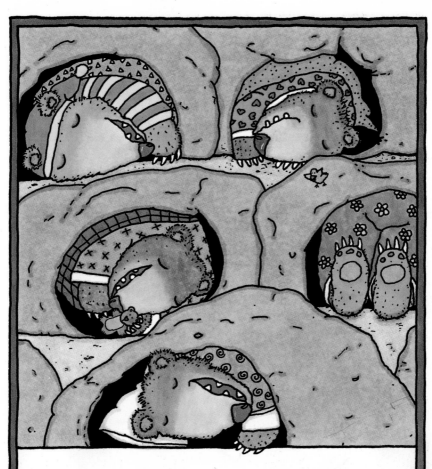

What country
do grizzlies like
to visit in the winter?

Den-mark!
It's known as the Hi-Bear Nation!

What muscleman do grizzlies most admire?

Conan the Bar-bear-ian!

How many campers
can a grizzly eat
on an empty stomach?

Just one—
after that his stomach isn't empty!

What grizzly has bad breath,
long, yellow teeth, mean
little eyes, and needs a bath?

A perfectly normal grizzly!

Who is the only one
that remembers grizzlies
at Christmas?

Santa Claws!

What do bears
think of these jokes?

They think they're just grisly!